Christmas 2020

To Gmara.

Happy Reading

Love,
Nanny, Poppy &
Auntie Jillia XO

FINDING CHRISTMAS

by **Robert Munsch**

illustrated by **Michael Martchenko**

North Winds Press
An Imprint of Scholastic Canada Ltd.

The illustrations in this book were painted in watercolour
on illustration board.
The type is set in 20 point ITC Century Book.

Library and Archives Canada Cataloguing in Publication

Munsch, Robert N., 1945-
Finding Christmas / by Robert Munsch ; illustrated by
Michael Martchenko.

ISBN 978-1-4431-1317-5

I. Martchenko, Michael II. Title.

PS8576.U575F47 2012   jC813'.54   C2012-901656-X

www.scholastic.ca

11 10 9 8 7   Printed in Malaysia 108   20 21 22 23 24

*For Julie, Andrew and
Tyya Munsch,
Guelph, Ontario*

Julie always found her Christmas presents.
One year she found them in the basement.
One year she found them in the bathroom.
One year she found them in the garage.

But THIS Christmas, Julie began to wonder if she was getting any presents from her family at all. She had looked and looked and looked and looked and found nothing.

On Christmas Eve, Julie decided to give it one last try.

She went down into the basement and pushed her way through spider webs.

NO PRESENTS!

She went into the bathroom and pulled out all the towels.

NO PRESENTS!

She went into her parents' bedroom and took all the clothes out of all the drawers, and all the clothes out of all the closets.

NO PRESENTS!

She moved everything out of the garage and looked underneath the car and behind the lawnmower.

NO PRESENTS!

She called her friend who lived across the street and said, "Denise, Denise! I have looked all over the house. There is nothing here! It is Christmas Eve and there are NO PRESENTS!

"None at all.

"NO PRESENTS!"

Denise said, "Stop! Stop! I am looking over at your house and guess what I see on the roof?"

"I know!" said Julie. "There is a Santa Claus with a sleigh. My mom and dad put that up this year. Isn't it neat?"

"Yes, it is neat," said Denise. "And what is in the back of the sleigh on top of your roof?"

"A large box!" said Julie.

"Yes!" said Denise. "And what do you think is in the box?"

"Of course!" said Julie. "They hid the presents on the roof!"

So Julie went to bed early, and then, very quietly, she climbed up onto the roof. She opened the top of the box and looked in.

The box was full of presents.

Julie pulled herself up . . . and fell in.

The top closed and she could not get out.

She yelled, "Denise!" But Denise had already gone to bed.

Julie yelled, "Daddy!" But her dad was busy decorating the tree.

She yelled, "Mommy!" But her mom was busy wrapping one last Christmas present for her dad.

She yelled, "Andrew!" But her brother was putting out a plate of cookies for Santa.

Julie even yelled, "Tyya!" But her sister had gone to sleep on the couch.

There was no way to get out, so Julie decided to take a nap.

She lay down in the middle of the presents, wrapped herself in a blanket and went to sleep.

Very late that night, Julie's mom and dad went up onto the roof, got the box and took it inside.

"Ha!" said Julie's dad. "Julie never saw any Christmas presents this time. She doesn't know what she's getting."

"Yes," said her mom, "we definitely fooled her this time."

They reached in the box and brought out
a bicycle.

"A great present for Andrew!" said Julie's dad.

They reached in the box and brought out
some markers.

"A great present for Julie!" said her mom.

They reached in the box and brought out
some building blocks.

"A great present for Tyya!" said her dad.

Then they reached in the box and brought
out . . . Julie, fast asleep.

"Look at this!" said Julie's dad. "It's a little
girl. Who's getting a little girl?"

"I didn't get anyone a little girl," said Julie's mom.

"Well, it looks like a really nice little girl, and I want it for MY Christmas present," said her dad.

"It looks like a really nice little girl to me, too, and I want it for MY Christmas present," said her mom.

"No," said her dad. "I saw it first and it's going to be MY present."

"No," said her mom. "It's a girl, and I'm a girl, so it should belong to me."

Then Julie woke up.

"Wait a minute," she said. "I belong to you both."

"Right," said her mom and dad. Then they gave her kisses and hugs and wrapped her up and put her under the Christmas tree with a label that said:

TO MOMMY AND DADDY.

On Christmas morning, Andrew and Tyya found Julie all wrapped up under the tree.

So Andrew wrapped himself up and went under the tree.

And Tyya wrapped herself up and went under the tree.

When their parents finally woke up, the kids all yelled, "Merry Christmas!"

And everyone agreed that it was the best Christmas ever.

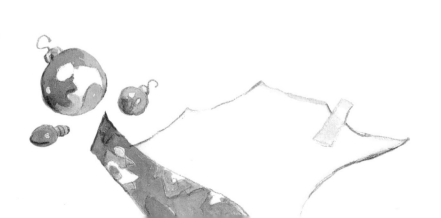